First published 1993 by Walker Books Ltd
87 Vauxhall Walk, London SE11 5HJ

This edition published 2009

2 4 6 8 10 9 7 5 3 1

This book has been typeset in Garamond Educational

Printed in China

British Library Cataloguing in Publication Data:
a catalogue record for this book is available from the British Library.

ISBN 978-0-7445-2638-7

www.walker.co.uk

Here come the Tiddlers

Catherine and Laurence Anholt

WALKER BOOKS
AND SUBSIDIARIES

LONDON · BOSTON · SYDNEY · AUCKLAND

We are the tiddlers...

tipple

topple,

topsy

turvy,

tiddlers are all round and curvy.

Tiddlers come in different sizes...

I am big,   we are small,

I am hardly here at all.

They are all different...

I am sleepy,

I am grumpy,

I am noisy,

I am jumpy,

I am sad,   I am happy,

I want Mum to change my nappy.

Tiddlers love to play...

up and down,

roundabout,

upside-down,

in and out.

Tiddlers can...

hop like a rabbit,

bark like a dog,

climb like a bear,

jump like a frog.

Tiddlers make lots of noise...

dancing,

singing,

banging,

ringing.

Tiddlers like eating...

I like jam,

we like bread,

I like jelly on my head.

Tiddlers are always busy...

crawling,

sitting,

peeping,

walking,   running,

sleeping.